randomhousekids.com
dianemuldrow.com

ISBN 978-0-7364-3425-6 (trade) — ISBN 978-0-7364-3426-3 (ebook)
PRINTED IN CHINA
10 9 8 7 6 5 4 3 2 1

Random House Children's Books supports the First Amendment and celebrates the right to read.

Everything I Need to Know I Learned From a

Disney

Little Golden Book

DIANE MULDROW

A GOLDEN BOOK • NEW YORK

Does your life seem more "ho-hum" . . .

From Walt Disney's *Snow White and the Seven Dwarfs*, illustrated by the Walt Disney Studio,
adapted by Ken O'Brien and Al Dempster, illustrated by the Walt Disney Studio, undated.

than "heigh-ho"?

Perhaps you've been feeling lethargic for what seems like a hundred years . . .

From Walt Disney's *Sleeping Beauty*, a Golden Tell-a-Tale Book, pictures by the Walt Disney Studio, adapted by Norm McGary, copyright MCMLIX (1959).

or you're unsure of your direction in life.

Maybe you're not thrilled with what the mirror's been telling you lately?

**Perhaps you're
a bit lonely,**

From Disney/Pixar *Ratatouille* by Victoria Saxon,
illustrated by Scott Tilley and Jean-Paul Orpiñas,
copyright 2007.

or you're thinking that your true love should have found you by now.

Don't panic.

From Walt Disney's *Alice in Wonderland,* illustrated by the Walt Disney Studio, adapted by Al Dempster from the motion picture, copyright 1951, 2010.

All you need is a little magic in your life!

From Walt Disney's *Little Man of Disneyland*, told by Annie North Bedford, illustrated by the Walt Disney Studio, adapted by Dick Kelsey, copyright 1955.

The good news is that having a genie or a fairy godmother is optional . . .

because magic is all around us!

From Walt Disney's *Grandpa Bunny*, told by Jane Werner, illustrated by the Walt Disney Studio,
adapted by Dick Kelsey and Bill Justice from the motion picture *Funny Little Bunnies*, copyright 1951, 2007.

Think back to when you heard stories of fairies and pirates

From Walt Disney's *Peter Pan and Wendy*, told by Annie North Bedford, illustrated by the Walt Disney Studio, adapted by Eyvind Earle, copyright 1952.

and far-off places,

From Disney's *Aladdin: The Magic Carpet Ride*, adapted by Teddy Slater Margulies,
illustrated by Kenny Thompkins, painted by Gary Eggleston, copyright 1993.

# of wizards
and castles

From Walt Disney's *The Wizards' Duel* told by Carl Memling, based on
the motion picture *The Sword in the Stone*, illustrated by the Walt Disney
Studio, adapted by Al White and Hawley Pratt, copyright 1963.

and wishes

coming true,

when you dreamed
of true love

and happily-ever-after,

and anything seemed possible.

From Walt Disney's *Peter Pan*, illustrated by
the Walt Disney Studio, adapted by John Hench
and Al Dempster, copyright 1952, 2007.

Hold those dreams close!
They can still come true.

Magic is something we can make ourselves!

From Walt Disney's *The Sorcerer's Apprentice*, adapted by Don Ferguson, illustrated by Peter Emslie, copyright 1994.

Start with a friend, a true-Baloo friend.

Add music and dancing,

perhaps a little romancing . . .

From Walt Disney's *Lady and the Tramp*,
adapted by Teddy Slater, illustrated by Bill Langley and Ron Dias, copyright 2012.

a star to wish on,

**and hope
in your heart.**

Life isn't always fair,

From Walt Disney's *The Sword in the Stone*, adapted by Carl Memling,
illustrated by the Walt Disney Studio, adapted by Norm McGary, copyright 1963.

and mean girls

and bullies seem to be everywhere.

From Disney's *Beauty and the Beast: The Teapot's Tale*, adapted by Justine Korman,
illustrated by Peter Emslie and Darren Hunt, copyright 1993.

Don't despair.

Just keep swimming!

Eventually you'll come up into the sunshine.

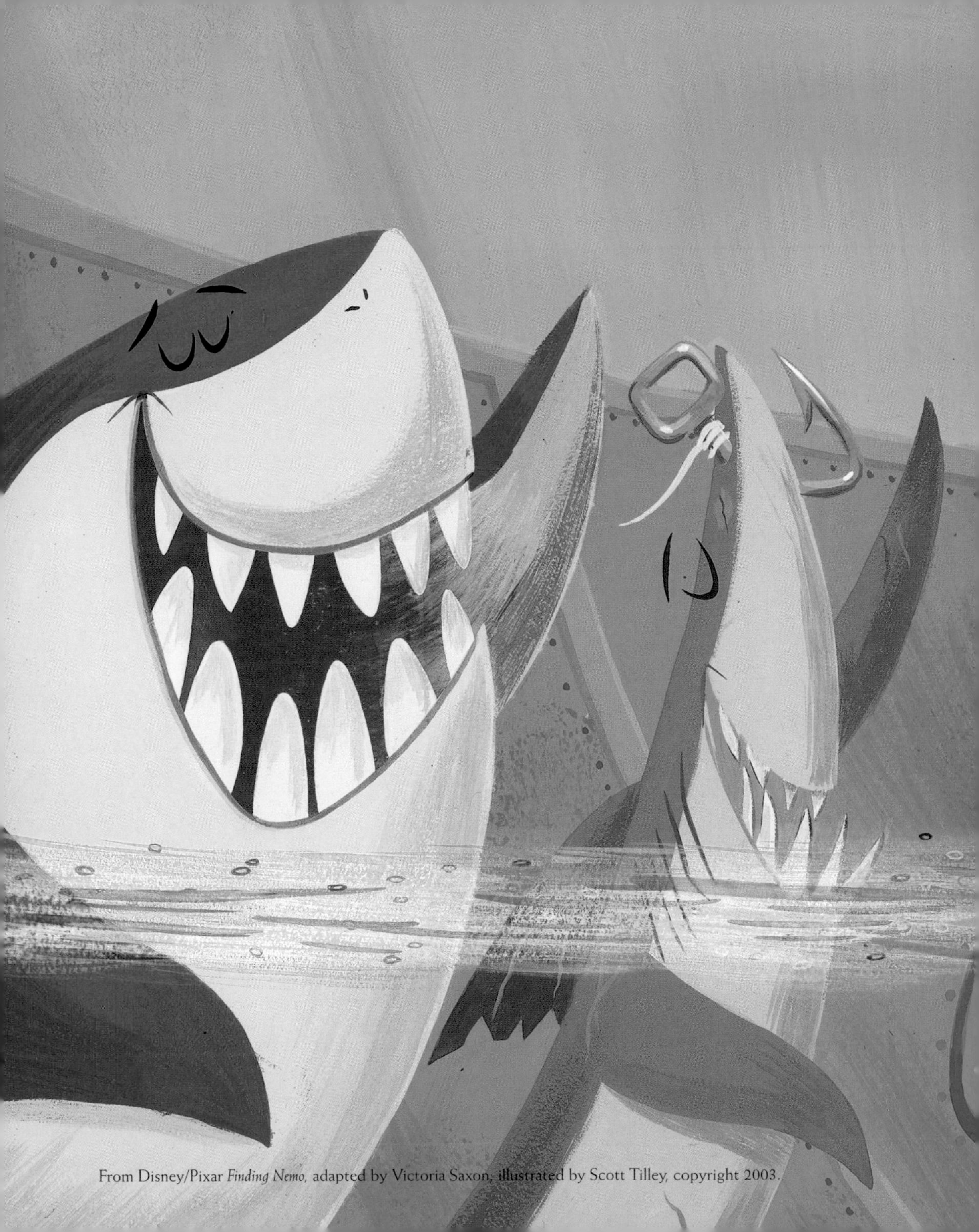

With hope in your heart,
you can swim with the sharks

(or whales).

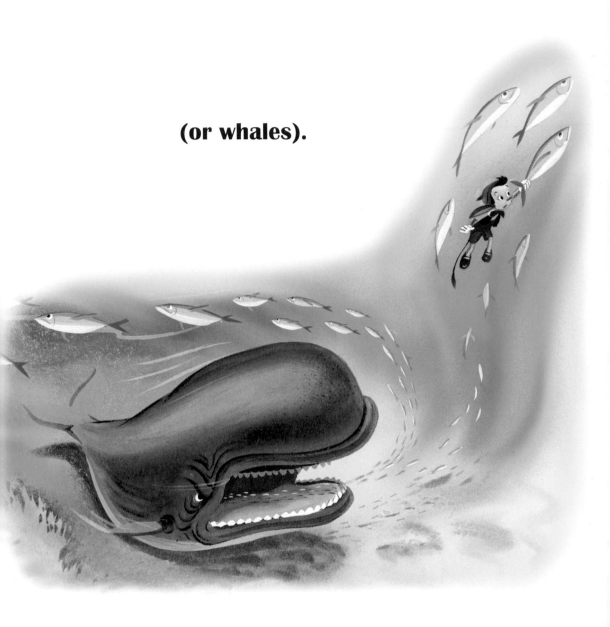

You can tap into your inner warrior to do what's right.

But there would be no magic without your love—and its power.

Love can bloom in the most desolate places.

From Disney/Pixar *Wall•E*, adapted by Vick•E,
illustrated by Jean-Paul Orpiñas and Scott Tilley, copyright 2008.

It gives us courage,

it overcomes evil,

From Walt Disney's *Sleeping Beauty*, told by Annie North Bedford, illustrated by the Walt Disney Studio, adapted by Julius Svendsen, Frank Armitage, and Walt Peregoy, copyright 1957.

and it endures,

because love is stronger than hate.

So keep your heart open,

and look for the beauty in others. . . .

New friends are waiting in the wings for you,

ready to share wonderful times.

For there's no one quite like you

and what you bring to the picture.

From Disney/Pixar *Monsters, Inc.*, adapted by Andrea Posner-Sanchez, illustrated by the Disney Storybook Artists, copyright 2012.

We're all born with certain gifts and talents.

So use what you've got!

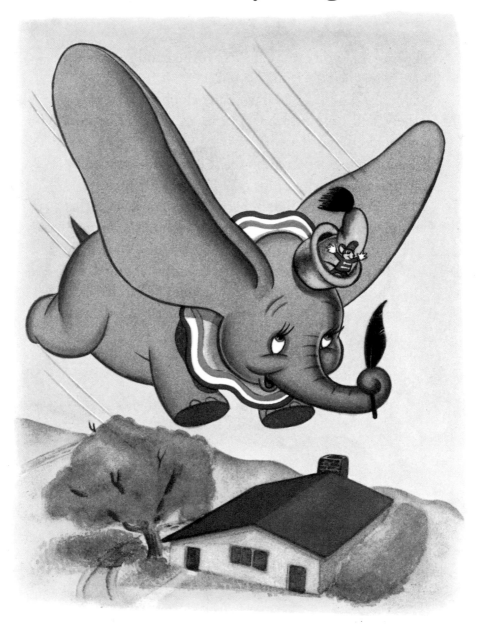

Show your moxie . . .

and take your place at the ball!

(It wouldn't be as exciting without you.)

From Walt Disney's *Cinderella*, adapted by Jane Werner,
illustrated by Retta Scott Worcester, copyright 1950.

The world needs
your own particular magic!

From Disney *Frozen*, adapted by Victoria Saxon,
illustrated by Grace Lee, Massimiliano Narciso,
and Andrea Cagol, copyright 2014.

Claim your rightful place in the world—

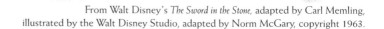

From Walt Disney's *The Sword in the Stone*, adapted by Carl Memling, illustrated by the Walt Disney Studio, adapted by Norm McGary, copyright 1963.

your destiny awaits!

From Disney's *The Lion King*, adapted by Justine Korman,
illustrated by Don Williams and H. R. Russell, copyright 1994.

Life really is
a journey

and a gift.

And it's a super-cali-fragi-listic new day!

Jump in!

And see what's waiting for you
on the other side.

From Disney/Pixar *Ratatouille* by Victoria Saxon,
illustrated by Scott Tilley and Jean-Paul Orpiñas, copyright 2007.

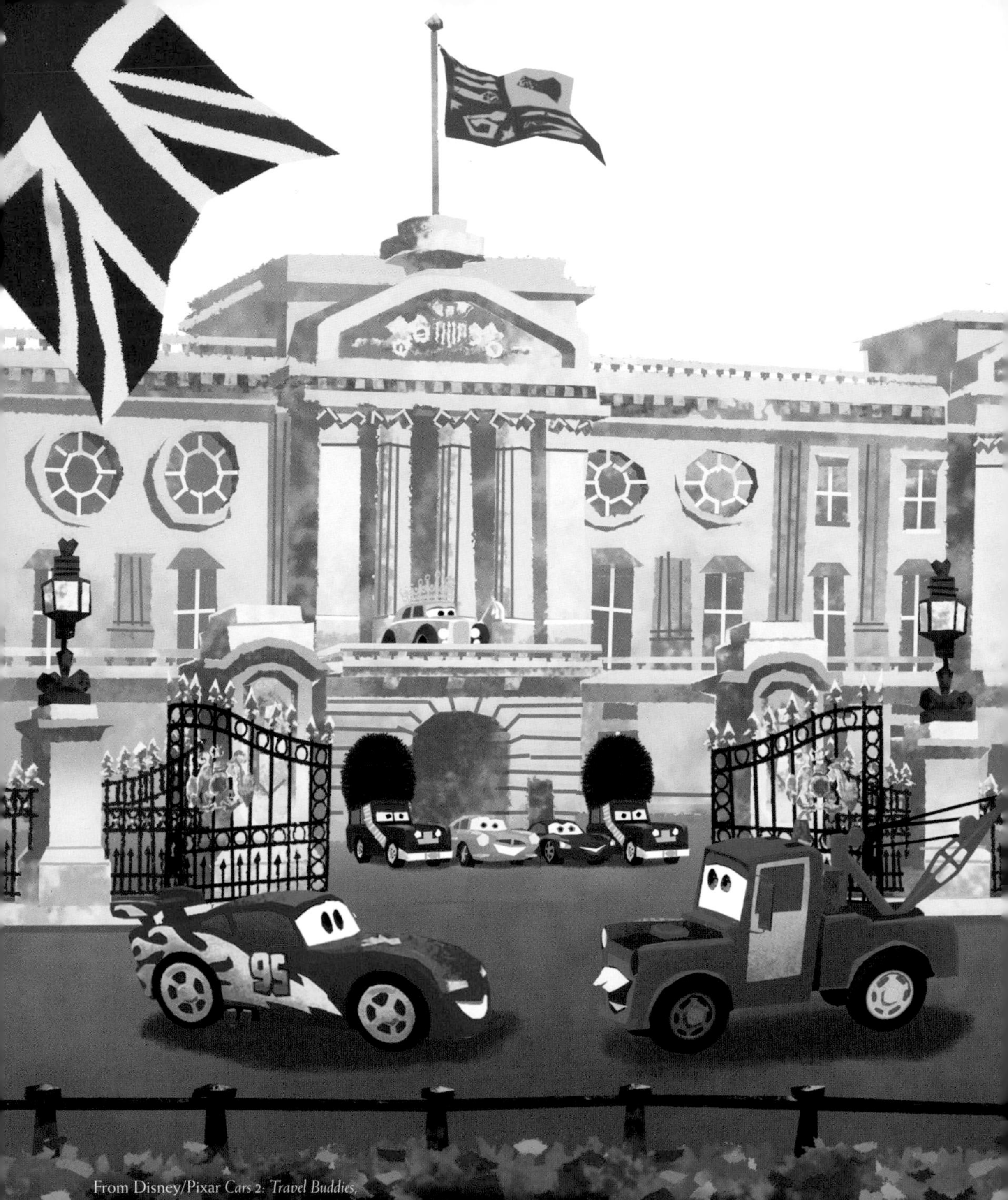

From Disney/Pixar *Cars 2: Travel Buddies,*
illustrated by Andrew Jimenez, Harley Jessup, and Jason Merck, copyright 2012.

The world is full of
magical places.

Be curious,

be an explorer.

From Disney Princess *The Little Mermaid*, a Big Golden Book, adapted by Barbara Bazaldua, illustrated by the Disney Storybook Artists, copyright 2013.

Warning: your journey may take you out of your comfort zone!

Do it anyway.

Look up,

and listen,

and watch for doors
that are opening for you.

From Walt Disney's *Alice in Wonderland: Mad Hatter's Tea Party*, retold by Jane Werner, illustrated by the Walt Disney Studio, adapted by Richmond I. Kelsey and Don Griffith, copyright 1951.

Are you ready to make your own magic?

It's up to you!

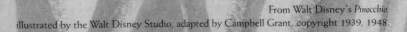

From Walt Disney's *Pinocchio*,
illustrated by the Walt Disney Studio, adapted by Campbell Grant, copyright 1939, 1948.

Soon you'll see your dreams coming true!